SHARE SAID THE ROOSTER

Pamela Allen

PENGUIN|VIKING

For Thomas and Toby to share

VIKING

Published by the Penguin Group
Penguin Group (Australia)
250 Camberwell Road, Camberwell, Victoria 3124, Australia
(a division of Pearson Australia Group Pty Ltd)
Penguin Group (USA) Inc.
375 Hudson Street, New York, New York 10014, USA
Penguin Group (Canada)
90 Eglinton Avenue East, Suite700,
Toronto ON M4P 2Y3, Canada
(a division of Pearson Penguin Canada Inc.)
Penguin Books Ltd
80 Strand, London WC2R 0RL, England
Penguin Ireland
25 St Stephen's Green, Dublin 2, Ireland
(a division of Penguin Books Ltd)
Penguin Books India Pvt Ltd
11 Community Centre, Panchsheel Park, New Delhi – 110 017, India
Penguin Group (NZ)
Cnr Airborne and Rosedale Roads, Albany, Auckland, New Zealand
(a division of Pearson New Zealand Ltd)
Penguin Books (South Africa) (Pty) Ltd
24 Sturdee Avenue, Rosebank, Johannesburg 2196, South Africa

Penguin Books Ltd, Registered Offices: 80 Strand, London, WC2R 0RL, England

First published by Penguin Group (Australia), a division of Pearson Australia Group Pty Ltd, 2006

10 9 8 7 6 5 4 3 2 1

Copyright © Pamela Allen, 2006

The moral right of the author/illustrator has been asserted

Designed by Deborah Brash © Penguin Group (Australia)
Typeset in 24/32pt Tribute by Deborah Brash
Printed and bound by Imago Productions, China

National Library of Australia
Cataloguing-in-Publication data:

   Allen, Pamela.
   'Share,' said the Rooster.

   ISBN 0670029424

   I. Title.

A823.3

www.puffin.com.au

Here are five little stories of two little men,
one called Billy and one called Ben.

This is story number one
of the two little men
and a pink sticky bun.

'Share,' said the rooster.
'Share,' said the hen.

'No,' cried Billy.

'No,' cried Ben.

And that's the sad story
of these two little men.

This is story number two
of the two little men
and boots painted blue.

'Share,' said the rooster.
'Share,' said the hen.

'No,' cried Billy.

'No,' cried Ben.

And that's the sad story
of these two little men.

This is story number three
of the two little men
and an apple up a tree.

'Share,' said the rooster.
'Share,' said the hen.

'No,' cried Billy.

'No,' cried Ben.

And that's the sad story
of these two little men.

This is story number four
of the two little men
when it started to pour.

'Share,' said the rooster.
'Share,' said the hen.

'No,' cried Billy.

'No,' cried Ben.

And that's the sad story
of these two little men.

This is story number five
when the two little men
nearly lost their lives.

'Share,' said the rooster.
'Share,' said the hen.

'No,' cried Billy.

'No,' cried Ben.

And that's the last story
of these two little men.
Goodbye Billy. Goodbye Ben.